Put Beginning Readers on the Right Track with
ALL ABOARD READING™

The All Aboard Reading series is especially for beginning readers. Written by noted authors and illustrated in full color, these are books that children really and truly *want* to read—books to excite their imagination, tickle their funny bone, expand their interests, and support their feelings. With four different reading levels, All Aboard Reading lets you choose which books are most appropriate for your children and their growing abilities.

Picture Readers—for Ages 3 to 6
Picture Readers have super-simple texts, with many nouns appearing as rebus pictures. At the end of each book are 24 flash cards—on one side is the rebus picture; on the other side is the written-out word.

Level 1—for Preschool through First-Grade Children
Level 1 books have very few lines per page, very large type, easy words, lots of repetition, and pictures with visual "cues" to help children figure out the words on the page.

Level 2—for First-Grade to Third-Grade Children
Level 2 books are printed in slightly smaller type than Level 1 books. The stories are more complex, but there is still lots of repetition in the text, and many pictures. The sentences are quite simple and are broken up into short lines to make reading easier.

Level 3—for Second-Grade through Third-Grade Children
Level 3 books have considerably longer texts, harder words, and more complicated sentences.

All Aboard for happy reading!

Great galloping gumballs! This book is for my
special friends Sjors, Alice, Anneke, Gretchen,
and Sjardo Steneker—M.V.

To my brother Raymond—T.P.

Based on GOLDSWORTHY AND MORT in *Summer Fun*, published by HarperCollins
Canada, Toronto. Copyright © 1990 by Marcia Vaughan.

Text copyright © 1999 by Marcia Vaughan. Illustrations copyright © 1999 by Thomas Payne.
All rights reserved. Published by Grosset & Dunlap, Inc., a member of Penguin Putnam
Books for Young Readers, New York. ALL ABOARD READING is a trademark of The
Putnam & Grosset Group. GROSSET & DUNLAP is a trademark of Grosset & Dunlap, Inc.
Published simultaneously in Canada. Printed in the U.S.A.

Library of Congress Cataloging-in-Publication Data

Vaughan, Marcia K.
   The lemonade stand / by Marcia Vaughan ; illustrated by Thomas Payne.
     p. cm. — (All aboard reading. Level 1)
   Summary: Two animal friends plan to make money at their lemonade stand, but find
that selling can be thirsty work.
   [1. Animals—Fiction. 2. Moneymaking projects—Fiction.]
   I. Payne, Thomas, ill. II. Title. III. Series.
   PZ7.V452Le   1999   98-49203
   [E]—dc21   CIP
                                                        AC

ISBN 0-448-41977-7   A B C D E F G H I J

ALL
ABOARD
READING™

Level 1
Preschool-Grade 1

LEMONADE STAND

By Marcia Vaughan
Illustrated by Tom Payne

Grosset & Dunlap • New York

It was a hot summer day.
Boomer and Squeak set up
their lemonade stand.

"Lots of animals will want
lemonade today,"
Boomer said.

"Soon our jars
will be full of money.
We will be rich."

"Good," said Squeak.

"I will buy a boat.

A blue boat with red sails."

"I will buy a sports car,"
Boomer said.
"A yellow sports car
with a loud horn
and shiny wheels."

Squeak stood on his chair
and looked around.

He did not see anyone.

"I wonder who will buy
the first glass," he said.

SQUEAK

"I will," said Boomer.

Boomer took a nickel
from his pocket.
He put it in Squeak's jar.
Squeak gave him
a glass of lemonade.
"This is good," said Boomer.
"Try some."

So Squeak took the nickel
out of his jar.
He put it in Boomer's jar.
"We have sold two glasses,"
said Boomer.
"We are getting richer."

Boomer and Squeak

sat and sat.

They waited and waited.

Nobody came.

"All this sitting and waiting makes me thirsty," said Squeak.

"Let me buy you a drink,"
said Boomer.
Boomer took the nickel
out of his jar.
He put it in Squeak's jar.
He gave his friend a drink.

"Yum," said Squeak.

"May I return the favor?"
Squeak handed the nickel
back to Boomer.

He gave Boomer a drink.

Boomer and Squeak sat
and waited some more.
"Maybe nobody knows
we are here," Squeak said.
"I will carry our sign around."

Squeak ran across
the bridge,

around the lake,

over the hill,
and back.

"Did you find any thirsty animals?"

Boomer asked.

Squeak huffed and puffed.

"Yes, I did," panted Squeak.

"Me! May I borrow five cents?"

Boomer took the nickel

out of his jar

and handed it to Squeak.

Squeak took a glass of lemonade

and gulped it down.

Boomer held up the pitcher.
"Now we have only one glass
of lemonade left," he said.
Squeak looked worried.

"What if two animals
   want lemonade?" he asked.
"They might fight.
   Quick, Boomer!
   Drink the last glass!"

Boomer did just that.

"The lemonade is gone,"
Boomer said.

"We must be rich.

Let's count our money."

BOOMER

5¢

Boomer and Squeak
shook their jars.
One shiny nickel rolled across
the table.
"Great gumballs!" said Boomer.
"We have made only five cents!"

"You cannot buy a boat
  with five cents," said Squeak.
"Or a sports car," said Boomer.

"There is only one thing
you can buy for five cents,"
said Squeak.
Boomer and Squeak
took their nickel.

They ran across the bridge,
around the lake,
over the hill, and all the way
to Mrs. Pip's store.

"What would you like?"
asked Mrs. Pip.
Boomer and Squeak
smiled and said,
"One glass of lemonade, please!"